Praise for
Crazy LIttle Thing Called

MW00933751

"This is the best-damned book I've seen in years. Laughing out loud at these intelligent cartoons was a truly guilty pleasure. If irreverence is a virtue, Graham Sale is a saint."
- *Dan Barker, co-president of the Freedom From Religion Foundation and author*

"Graham's book once again bears witness to his wonderfully offbeat sense of humor as he unerringly and brilliantly skewers evangelicals, proselytizers, God, the Bible, the Ten Commandments, pedophile priests, Donald Trump, and people who believe that America was founded as a Christian nation. A breath of fresh air in a world suffering from religious intolerance, jingoism, male chauvinism, and a growing need to maintain a clear separation of church and state."
- *Steve Salemson, Retired Scholarly Publisher and Unabashed Atheist*

"Helluva godless good read. WARNING: Do not open if you believe in the Wizard of Oz."
Steve Benson, Pulitzer-Prize Winning Editorial Cartoonist emeritus at the Arizona Republic

"God help us. The Lenny Bruce of religion has been unleashed on mankind."
—*Graham Halky, VP of Creative Services, KVP, Inc.*

"Graham's book is irresistible. You will laugh, giggle and groan, even in inappropriate places. But like a good skeptic, don't take my word for it, use whatever free will you have left in this crazy world and grab a copy or two. This is one book you really can judge by its cover."
—*Chris Highland, former minister, author of A Free Thinker's Gospel and Life After Faith*

"Blessed are the meek: for they shall inherit the earth."
—*Bible, Mathew 5:5*

**"You have heard that it was said, 'An eye for an eye and a tooth for a tooth.'
But I say to you, Do not resist the one who is evil.** If anyone slaps you on
the right cheek, turn to him the other cheek also."
—*Bible, Mathew 5:38-39*

**"But I say to you who hear, Love your enemies, do good to those who hate you,
bless those who curse you, pray for those who abuse you.** To one who strikes you
on the cheek, offer the other also, and from one who takes away your cloak
do not withhold your tunic either."
—*Bible, Luke 6:27-29,*

**"Religion is excellent for keeping common people quiet.
Religion is what keeps the poor from murdering the rich."**
—*Napoleaon Bonaparte*

"Ungodly funny."
- *The Big Cheese*

More Praise for Graham's Cartoons

"Graham's cartoons are wonderfully inventive and he shares his world with us in so many ways. He can be wacky, clever, and often poetic. Something for everyone!"
- *Liza Donnelly, New Yorker cartoons, TED speaker, Forbes writer*

"Graham's cartoons and wit make me grin, wince, groan and giggle. I'm never sure what to expect from his twisted, sardonic mind except coffee-spitting entertainment. Sure, he has light moments, but it's his down and dirty satire that keeps me coming back for more!"
- *Sandee Beyerle, Managing Editor, Funny Times*

"Graham Sale's cartoons are crispy, pithy, surprising, elegant, tasty, sophisticated, stylish, clever, beautiful, provocative, pertinent, outrageous, timely, perceptive, revolutionary, and above all, absolutely hilarious!"
- *Randall Enos, National Lampoon, New York Times, The Nation, Rolling Stone, The Atlantic*

"I bought your cartoon book yesterday. I had to put my dog down this weekend. It has been a very sad time for me. But, your book has made me laugh so hard I cried tears of joy too. Thank you for sharing your talent and making me smile. I am going through it slowly because each one makes me laugh so hard I get side cramps. Thank you so much!"
- *Kelly Lehman, TN*

First Printing 2020
ISBN: 9798637000746
Little Black Book Press

**TO BUY THIS BOOK or
CONTACT GRAHAM:**
w) **www.grahamsale.com**
e) **graham@grahamsale.com**

PURCHASE THESE CARTOONS
and others on greeeting cards, mugs,
art prints, t-shirts and more on his website!

Crazy Little Thing Called Love

God & Religion
by GRAHAM SALE

WWW.GRAHAMSALE.COM

My father, Ed Sale, and me, outside the church where he was the minister in Elmira, NY.

Circa 1967

Circa 1965

Virginia Sale, my mother, who continues to spend endless hours, helping me understand life and dealing with a world filled with nincompoops.

INTRODUCTION

This book is a collection of my cartoons on God and religion that I've drawn over the years. Some have been published by brave publishers and earned me plenty of hate mail. It is meant to be humorous, scathing, and hopefully at times thoughtful. And contrary to what some readers may think, I have nothing against religion or anyone's deeply held beliefs—unless, of course, they are used to harm others. Life is chaotic and uncertain and I understand that for believers, faith, and religion can provide comfort, security, and a feeling that there is a plan and purpose for their life beyond their secular existence.

Religious narratives are filled with unbelievable stories, assertions, and contradictions. I think most people of faith, with the exception of fundamentalists, recognize this and focus on the underlying messages of love and compassion for others that their faith asserts.

As a cartoonist and editorialist, I find humor in the incredible, the ridiculous, the inconsistencies, and pious hypocrisy that abounds in religion. And I feel compelled to ridicule the hypocrites, brain-washers, and charlatans who prey on people's circumstances, fears, and vulnerabilities for profit and power. They deserve to be exposed and chastised for the damage they inflict in the name of God—and with vigor and intensity. They are a clear and present danger to civilization and always have been.

My Experience of Religion
I have an unusual background. Both of my parents were Presbyterian ministers. They were scholarly, liberal social activists, who walked their talk and changed the quality of people's lives through their love, care, concern, and commitment to basic human rights and dignity. They followed Jesus' teaching to love your neighbor as yourself. And the most "religious" thing we did in our household was saying grace at meals. What was most important was how we treated others.

My parents didn't insist that my sister and I embrace their faith just because it was their faith. They simply taught us compassion for others by being examples of their faith in action. I was told that faith is a choice. It is a belief in something you can't see or prove. My parents weren't pious and didn't take the Bible literally. They taught its historical and political context and how to interpret and apply it in daily life. I was always aware that the Bible was a collection of stories written by people hundreds of years after Christ who had never even met him. There were times when congregants left the church because my father wouldn't tell them what to think. He wanted them to think for themselves and choose how to respond to situations based on their faith—which often proves difficult for people who desire rules and to be told what to think.

As I got older I learned to appreciate the benefits of fellowship; people coming together to support their shared struggle of living in an irrational world full of uncertainty, unfairness, inconsistency, intolerance, inexplicable cruelty, hypocrisy, and dealing with the dissimilar beliefs and values of other people.

Ultimately, I didn't subscribe to the mythology of Christianity and am not a believer. But, I am proud of the morals and values I received from my upbringing: fairness, compassion, tolerance, and treating others as you wish to be treated. Life is a mystery and being human is difficult and subject to vast inconsistencies. And as far as I'm concerned, whatever it takes to get you through it is fine by me.

But, when I learned that the Christian narrative had been recycled and was the basis of many previous religions, it was impossible to view it as more than a story comprised of allegories. Allegories are useful to teach children life lessons. But, as an adult, I didn't need religion to know the difference between right and wrong, love and hate, compassion and indifference. Faith isn't a prerequisite to practice kindness, tolerance, and morality.

Lastly

Many people are afraid to admit they don't believe in God because they're often suspected of having no morals and thought of as heretics. Nothing could be further from the truth. In America, not believing in a God or subscribing to religion makes it difficult if not impossible to even be elected to public office. It is a shame. And we're all aware that some of the most pious, self-righteous believers are also the most amoral, intolerant, self-serving people around and bear no witness to the tenets of their faith.

There are different names for non-believers: atheists, free-thinkers, humanists. Atheism is often incorrectly referred to as a belief—which it isn't. It's simply the absence of belief in God. That's it. It doesn't mean to be against God or religion. The word *heretic* is a Middle English term that is misused and has become synonymous with the idea of evil and the devil. But, the word heretic is derived from the Greek word *hairetikos* meaning "to choose." And in this case, it refers to people who, because of personal experience and through critical thought, have chosen not to believe in an invisible supreme being. It isn't an easy decision. It comes with consequences, because it goes against what the majority of the world and most people's families believe and hold sacred. Personally, I hold critical thought in high-esteem.

In America, it isn't the government's role to care if its citizens believe in a God or not. Our beliefs are our own prerogative and protected under the Constitution. But today, all branches of the government have steadily usurped this right and are leading us into a theocracy. We must be vigilant. We must protect our rights.

MORE ABOUT THIS BOOK

This is a collection of cartoons that I've drawn over the years, in a variety of styles. It includes a special BONUS SECTION at the end where you can see step-by-step how a cartoon is drawn and enjoy some funny stories about being a cartoonist. I hope you have as much fun reading this as I had creating it. *Now it's time for some fun!*

In the beginning...
When men were honest
with women.

"You're the only woman in the world for me."

Nature vs. Nurture

If everyone enters the world pure, innocent, and godless...

Then we're introduced to God and are suddenly impure, full of sin, and in need of his saving.

Wouldn't that mean the best most natural state of humanity is to be godless?

(Oh, crap. Someone who has put some thought into this.)

SALE

"And that people need to be saved from God—not by God?"

"*The less you know about our creation the better.*"

On the Sixth Day...

The games began.

"*I have nothing to wear.*"

THIS IS OUR COUNTRY - NOT YOUR CHURCH.

Interview with God:

"My last name isn't Damnit."

God: In Hindsight.

"You should run this by a focus group before signing off."

MEN IN HATS

Some things aren't as self-evident as you'd think.

God creates the Constitution.

The kid and I pulled an all nighter.

But I think you'll be pleased with it.

"And naturally skeptical."

The bright side of Atheism

Evangelical Christians, Latter Day Saints and Jehovah's Wittnesses race to baptize the first extra-terrestial.

MEN IN HATS

Mormons are not Christian.

They believe Joseph Smith, received God's word written on four, double-sided, gold plates, from an angel on a hill.

That's crazy. Everyone knows that Moses received God's word on two stone tablets, from a talking, burning bush, on a mountain.

Duh...

SALE

Mormons aren't Christian.

MEN IN HATS

GOP: "Respect a woman's body to decide."

"Hell Yes, Lou, you've got my vote!"

"Different pope. Same poop."

"*Forgive me, father, for the things I've done for a Klondike Bar.*"

"Tell an angry woman she's over-reacting. She will realize you're right and immediately calm down. That one didn't go over so well."

"Women have always had a time-honored place in our faith.
Right over there in the corner."

SALE

"Why do I attract so many crackpots?"

Defining Moments In Canine History.

And God said...

"You can have opposable thumbs and live independently, come and go as you please, and never rely on humans for all your needs."

"Or..."

"You can lick yourself."

The Immaculate Reflection.

"When they discovered I wasn't white, the shit hit the fan.
Being a short, pudgy, liberal Jew didn't work in my favor either."

The Heebie Gee Bees

"*Good evening goys and jews. The body has been placed inside the empty tomb and sealed with this ginormous boulder. Nothing can get in or out. I'm now going to wave my wand, say some magic words and we'll reassemble at sunrise to see what we find—or don't.*"

"Son, if you can make it there, you can make it anywhere."

"*My father is planning to kill me!*"

THE ANTI-PASTA

51

MEN IN HATS

Secular Divinity.

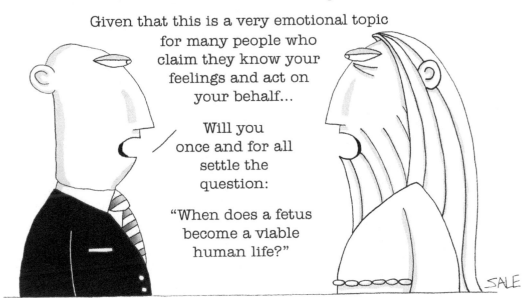

"When it pays off its student loans."

"*But, do you have a peanut for my friend?*"

Another day in Paradise.

God Creates Vengeance:

"Jury duty."

"This can't be good."

God goes on record:

If I can put pictures of my son and his mother on pancakes, potato chips and grilled cheese...

(Gulp.)

"You can sell cake to gays. Capiche?

"Boys are different from girls in many significant ways, and as you meet more of them, you'll discover that gay men are God's gift to women."

MEN IN HATS

What is the greatest threat to marriage?

Familiarity.
Boredom.
The internet.
Cellulite.
Back hair.
Monogamy.
Breasts.
Pornography.
Children.
Money.
In-laws
Gays.
The penis.

SALE

MEN IN HATS

Same-sex marrige kills.

MEN IN HATS

Republican "Open-Carry" Jesus.

Evangelicals.

We don't need to do anything to fix climate change.

You will save us.

"I gave you scientists, dumbass."

"How long can you tread water?"

MEN IN HATS

Back to basics.

Reformed Buddhists

Part 1. Mary & Joseph go to the "Antiques Road Show"

Unfortunately, frankincense and myrrh have little value today. However, had you kept the set intact and not traded the gold for cash we'd be talking seven figures—probably higher."

*"Naturally, preserving a historic item increases its value.
But good heavens! Bronzing the Messiah's baby sandals?
What on earth were you thinking?"*

Part 3. | Mary & Joseph Go Online.

"After two disappointing visits to the Antiques Road Show, Mary and Joseph met with a messiah memorabilia collector they found on Craigslist."

As first time offenders Mary and Joseph got off with probation, community service and parenting classes for keeping a child in a manger.

God relaxes with his laser pointer.

"He says those black holes in the time continuum are just him binge-watching cat videos and Netflix."

"Let's just say, it's not on his bucket list."

"No, I believe in an investment with a return."

Interview with God:

Do you have any advice for aspiring gods and prophets?

Publish or perish.

And of course...

"Never let the truth get in the way of a good story."

"*Blessed are those who aren't schmucks.*"

"It's fabulous!"

Religion for Dummies:

PAY ATTENTION.

Obama is not a Muslim.

Trump is not a Christian.

You are not a Christian.

You are a moron.

"You elect him President and claim I sent him."

"Listen up you babies. We fought hard for your right to be born—even killed for it — but, from now on you little moochers are on your own; especially you brown ones."

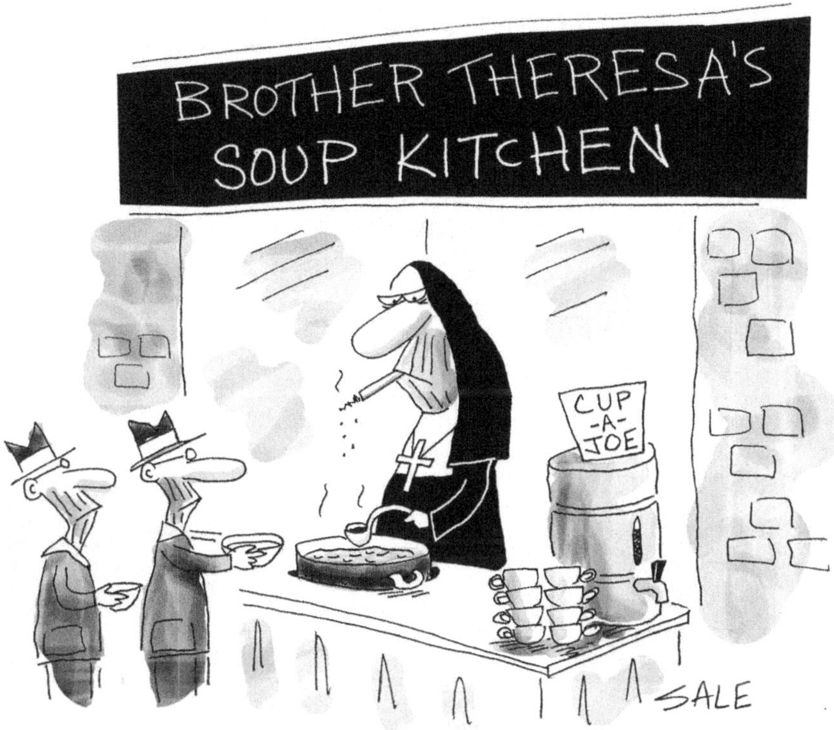
BROTHER THERESA'S
SOUP KITCHEN
CUP
-A-
JOE
SALE

"He made me an atheist."

"I'd like to take a moment to talk to you about Aquaman, our Lord and Savior."

War on Rainbows.

God created beautiful rainbows and their pretty colors for straight people.

But, the gays and undecideds have stolen them!

And left us with nothing but khaki.

"Amen, my straight white brother."

"If God hates gays, why does he let straight people keep making us?

"If they yell for me during sex, I know it's a false alarm and feel no obligation to ~~watch~~ respond—unless they're cute."

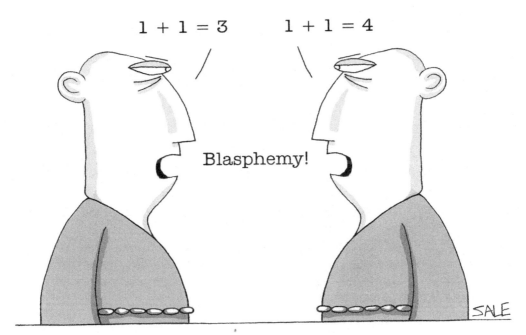

Religions Debate.

Evangelicals.

"Christianity isn't taught in church."

"I'm a religious extremist?"

INTERVIEW W/GOD: GOD REVEALS WHY POPE BENEDICT XVI LEFT...

YOU'LL LOVE THIS, JIMMY...
AS THE POPE WAS PRAYING
THE GAYS AWAY...

THEY WERE PRAYING
HIM AWAY!

MY PRAYER LINES
WERE ON FIRE!

I BET.

I'M FAMOUS FOR HYPOCRICY,
BUT EVEN I COULDN'T IGNORE THIS.
PLUS, THE NAZI THING HAD BEEN NAGGING
AT ME.

SOME FOLKS WILL FEEL
I STOPPED SHORT & SHOULD'VE
ENDED THE PAPACY ENTIRELY.

THAT'S
UNDERSTANDABLE.

SO, AS A COMPROMISE
I'M BRINGING BACK
THE McRIB.

THAT'S
A REAL
CROWD
PLEASER!

SALE

94

2:32 am

God postpones his most mundane chores.

Damn superstitious Catholics.

Time to make the Holy water.

"But it's Hell for skeptics."

God Blogs.

Spoiler Alert:

What's your position on evangelical, right-wing, conservative extremists, and billion dollar mega church types?

They are morally obese faith invaders...

"With unenviable futures."

"Everyone seems to find him there."

COMMENT

"I have spent the last thirty years studying and teaching the word of God. Your cartoon portraying the Lord Jesus Christ as a dark-skinned, foreign-born, anti-war liberal socialist who wants to give away health care and food to the masses in no way represents the Christ of the Bible. It is offensive. Socialism attempts to make government play the part of the Holy Spirit. There is not a single word in the Bible allowing charitable use of tax dollars. Socialism is anti-biblical."
–Pastor Franklin Washington, Memphis, TN

"You have a sick depraved mind and need counseling.
I know a Christian Counseling Center that can help you. I'll be praying for you.
There is a day of accountability and you need to prepare for it, Mr. Sale."
–Denise Macer, Cordova, TN

Over the years, I've received lots of hate mail from readers in response to my editorial cartoons. My MEN IN HATS, "Knock-Knock"cartoon received negative mail like these from self-descrlibed "Christians." I don't know what Bible these people follow, but it isn't one I am familiar with.

MEN IN HATS

Wrong. I'm Jesus Christ your savior. Get to know me.

MEN IN HATS

Attending church and quoting the Bible doesn't make you a Christian.

Baptism only declares your candidacy and intention to follow Christ. Only when you die and are judged by your actions will you learn if you were actually Christian and lived Christ-like.

Which is why it's hard to understand why some of you are so eager for Judgement Day...

Where you'll discover you did unto others as Satan would do not as Jesus said to do and you are going straight to Hell.

SALE

Spoiler Alert: To Religious Extremists.

Hell's Angels.

"And, it was nailed to the wall.
Now, that's Hell."

Parenting:

Dad...
I'm joing the
Peace Corps.

Your results may vary.

MEN IN HATS

Fundamentalists have a long history of disobeying God and perverting his message.

They disobeyed Him from the Beginning and were kicked out of Paradise. So, God gave them ten rules to live by —*in writing and in stone*—so they wouldn't forget or lose them. They ignored those too. And God destroyed the world.

However... Even that didn't stop them from violating his word.

Finally... God reduced his message. "Love your neighbor as yourself." Treat people decently and leave judgment up to Him. Then, he killed his son to make his point.

But true to form, they continue to ignore Him and do the exact opposite *and worse.*

SALE

If you don't believe in your own religion maybe it's time to get another.

"I created Hell."

"Finding guys named James, John, Mathew, Andrew, Paul, Timothy, Thomas, and Stephen, in the Middle East."

"Jesus loved the summer, but being a Messiah had its drawbacks."

MEN IN HATS

People who believe in God believe when they die they'll go to a glorious after-life far better than this one.

Some believe we're living in the End Times right now and can't wait to meet their Maker.

Atheists believe this ife is all there is and when they die they will be *leaving a glorious life.*

So, shouldn't politicians and military leaders be atheists...

Since they have more to live for?

SALE

A radical or reasonable thought? (Part 1.)

MEN IN HATS

A radical or reasonable thought? (Part 2.)

Holy Month-at-a Glance.

Jan.
Be everywhere.

Feb.
Be everywhere.

March.
Be everywhere...

SALE

God invents over-achievement.

"*You are everyone's emergency contact.*"

God calculates...

How much is too much to give his followers to handle.

A Modest Request:

Okay, I'll gladly believe in God: praise his name, give him my money, renounce logic, attend pot luck suppers, run his bingo parlors, and even teach Sunday school.

If, when I die...

"I'm put in charge of the Department of Karma."

"We're Cheesitarians. Have you heard the good news about the power of cheeses? Cheesus saves!"

War on Christmas.

"You need to work on your sales pitch."

God's Message to Fundamentalists.

You are out of your fucking mind if you you think...

"You're living with me for all eternity."

In Hindsight:

The "Bring Your Kid to Work" thing totally blindsided me.

Next thing I knew, JC was the Savior of the friggin' world.

"And let me tell you, he was pretty full of himself for quite some time. I started calling him Genghis Cohen."

Advances in forensic science bring scholars back to Jesus' tomb where they make surprising new discoveries.

Advances in forensic science bring scholars back to Jesus' tomb where they make surprising new discoveries.

Advances in forensic science bring scholars back to Jesus' tomb where they make surprising new discoveries.

The day after Jesus' birth an announcement was made throughout the land for people to change their calendars from B.C. to A.D..

MEN IN HATS

Once a year in the dark of night, the buck-toothed Easter Hare...

Snatches baskets full of unborn baby chicks from their mother's nest...

And takes them back to his den where he boils and tatoos them

Then, he hides them in people's lawns for children to hunt them and eat them *for fun.*

SALE

TALES FROM THE COOP.

"Want me to lay an egg right now? I will, no problem. You'll see."

MEN IN HATS

MEN IN HATS

God created the world, exactly as it is in six days.

Natural History museums are Satan's recruitment centers. Evolutionists claim animal and human DNA are practically the same. Well, if monkeys are our closest relative then why can't we eat bananas with our feet?

And without God, how do you explain America's greatness or...

Jesus and Mary appearing on potato chips and toast? *Hmmm?*

SALE

Creationists: Proof that evolution may only be a theory.

God's Message to His Followers.

Look,
I gave you
free will.

So,
please stop
pestering me
about my
"plan" for
you.

SALE

*"There-is-no-plan. And if you want a pony for
Christmas you'll have to buy it yourself."*

"Just nothing that involves you."

God: On the Record.

Is there anything you would like people to know that they would be surprised to learn about you?

Yes...

"I have never spoken to a politician. Not once. Not ever."

MEN IN HATS

Conservative Christian County Clerks say they'll go to jail before issuing same-sex marriage licenses...

Because it violates God's Law and their deeply held religious beliefs.

But, they have no problem giving licenses to liars, cheaters, adulterers, coveters, theives, murders, pedophiles...

Pork and shell fish eaters, non-believers, and other violators of God's Laws.

SALE

Deeply held beliefs also work in mysterious ways.

MEN IN HATS

A simple solution.

THE GAYS.

HI, WE'RE YOUR TYPICAL LIBERAL, ATHEIST, GAYS.

OR TURNING PEOPLE GAY, OR CAUSING RANDOM ACTS OF HORRIFIC VIOLENCE...

AND WHEN WE AREN'T CHANGING THE CLIMATE & CAUSING APOCALYPTIC WEATHER EVENTS...

WE ENJOY LOTS OF ANONYMOUS SEX, PROJECT RUNWAY & *BEING FABULOUS!*

SALE

"Or we couldn't a got married."

MEN IN HATS

"Correctamundo."

"I don't re-gift."

The Recession Hits Heaven.

SALE

With a soaring deficit and the high cost of energy, God is forced to review his policy of opening a window whenever closing a door.

"I'm not religious. I'm spiritual."

Early notes on creation.

MEN IN HATS

Evangelical preachers and conservative politicians are *fixated* on controlling everybody else's sex life.

They preach the sanctity of marriage and abstinence until marriage. They say gays are perverts and should be feared and despised.

But, what they really fear is having *their own* broken vows and perverted behavior discovered...

And being shamed and despised for their hypocricy and lies

SALE

"Evangenitals Mangled Moral Compass."

"If they love each other."

Mission Accomplished.

*"Sir, Hell is on line 666. They say the Bin Laden package
has arrived and they're already having fun with it."*

God invents prose:

(Sigh.)

Roses are Red. Silence is Golden. Duct tape is Gray. Chameleons are...

"Writing the Bible is gonna be a bitch."

MEN IN HATS

No representation without taxation.

"If contraception was retro-active—you'd be on death row."

"Care to guess what your chances for admittance are?"

MEN IN HATS

Before social media I assumed most people were reasonably intelligent, kind, decent, respectful folks...

Who believed in fairness, equality, math, science, and *live-and-let-live*. If my house caught fire they'd grab a hose and call the fire department.

I didn't think my neighbors had an arsenal of weapons in their basement or secretly hated me and think I'm going to Hell for what I believe—or don't.

And now, if my house catches fire there's a good chance they started it.

Ignorance was bliss.

SALE

The good old days.

"And fruitcakes like you."

"You don't see your co-worker Buddha's flock acting like hateful lunatics!"

Atheist
Hypocrite
If you can ignore parts of the Bible you don't like...
Why can't I ignore what I don't like?
Like all of it.
SALE

White House Committee on Science & Technology
United States of America, 21st Century. (Believe it or not.)

"Just because it's different from yours? And what do you think God has planned for you for screwing with his plan?"

God gets the last laugh.

"This is the operator. You have a collect call from Hell, from a Mr. Oral Roberts. Will you accept the charges?"

Pat Robertson makes God sick.

"Sht the hell up, you lunatic!"

The greatest Christian in America lobbying for religious support...

COVID-19

At first, I was like mask-shmask.
Wear one, don't wear one, whatever.

I'm the healthiest person in the world.
Why do I need one?

But, then my kid,
~~Brian~~ Baron, sent me
a memo saying the
fake news scared him.

So,
being the world's
greatest father
I thought,
why not?

"I want everyone to remember who to thank in November."

The End
is Near...

CARTOONIST

WWW.GRAHAMSALE.COM

Bonus Stuff...

CARTOONIST AT WORK.

Anatomy of a Cartoon

Ever wonder how an idea turns into a cartoon?
Well, here's an example of how it works for me...

After the underwear bomber tried to ignite his short-and-curlies, the TSA and airports worldwide began installing devices to see through people's clothes to discover what nefarious goodies they might be concealing. This outrageous invasion of privacy was fertile ground for cartoonists and comedians.

The following are sketches and notes I made while coming up with a cartoon on this issue.

My first thoughts were:
1) Could this lunatic's actions have an upside?

2) Would the fear of being seen naked by strangers in a public place make people get healthy and fit?

3) Would the Nigerian Crotch Rocket do for health and fitness what Jerrod did for *Subway* and the submarine sandwich?

4) **What less invasive ways** could be used to see into the hearts and minds of passengers to discover their intentions?

Other possible consequences:

5) Would lingerie/underwear stores and tanning/waxing salons suddenly appear in airports to help travelers look their best?

6) Would women rejoice because their husbands finally replace their raggedy old drawers?

7) Would the sudden attention to personal fitness and grooming cause marital riffs, since they're often signs of an affair?

8) Will gyms start offering "Boot Camps for Travelers?"

3 It was clear that several ideas had potential.

I decided to work on an image that would incorporate a few of the ideas. I returned to my first sketch and changed the perspective to read more quickly.

Then...
I redrew it over and over using a light box and I scanned it into photoshop to make final corrections and add shading until it felt finished...

And I did a second cartoon from my notes...

Who would want to take their phone with them everywhere?

You must be kidding.

In the early '80s, I did some cartoons for publications that made some pretty outrageous claims. For instance....

An article I worked on claimed that telephones would soon be so small that we would take them with us wherever we went---it'd be as normal as putting on your hat and coat when leaving the house. *You must be kidding.* Who would want their phone with them all the time and constantly be interrupted by calls? With answering machines, pagers and pay phones on every corner, this sounded crazy and totally unnecessary to me. *Good luck with that idea, guys.*

Another job I worked on predicted that everyone would have at least one or more computers at work, at home---even in the *kitchen.* And someday they'd be small enough to carry in a briefcase. Not only that, but instead of going to the store we'd shop on our computer. *Say, what?*

Computers were expensive. Almost no one except big companies, law enforcement, NASA and the government had computers.

Computers were gigantic and cost as much as a house. The operating system was DOS, a black screen with sci-fi computer type. So, it was impossible to imagine it looking like a store where you'd want to shop. Moreover, how would products get inside your computer in the first place? And how would you put money in it to pay for stuff?

Remember, the internet didn't exist. ATMs were just being tested and fax machines were like magic---how did images on paper travel through the telephone? Can you imagine how futuristic this sounded?

I'd only seen computers on TV — so, when the editor sent me a photo of what a "desk top" computer looked like, I didn't know what I was looking at. I thought the monitor was the actual computer.

An Interview with Graham.

Sandee Beyerle, the managing editor of *Funny Times*, caught up with Graham Sale for a rarely insightful interview. Here are some excerpts.

SB: It's really great to finally meet you after all these years.
GS: I know, and this is going to be fun.
SB: I think so too. Are you ready to spill all?
GS: I'll do my best. And thank you for bringing this delicious box of wine.
SB: Nothing but the best for a cartoonist of your stature.

SB: So, where are you from?
GS: I was born in Detroit, MI where I was adopted by my wonderful parents, Ed and Virginia Sale. When I was three we moved to Elmira, NY where I grew up.

SB: Tell me about Elmira.

GS: It's a small town in western NY, near Corning and Ithaca. Some facinating people come from Elmira. Mark Twain lived, married, wrote and is buried there. Plus, Hal Roach, who produced *The Little Rascals* and *Laurel and Hardy*; Brian Williams, the anchorman; Ernie Davis, the first African-American to win a Heisman trophy; Eileen Collins, the first woman to command the Space Shuttle and Tommy Hilfiger was my neighbor.

...Continued.

SB: Is anyone else in your family an artist?
GS: No, both my father and mother were Presbyterian ministers. But, my biological mother and her mother were artistic.

SB: Aha! You're a preacher's kid. That explains everything. So why cartooning?
GS: I ask myself that all the time. I've always drawn, but I've never "always wanted to be a cartoonist." As a kid I wanted to be either Jim Henson, Sid or Marty Krofft or play for the NY Giants. Then, when I discovered girls, there was no doubt in my mind that being a Playboy photographer was the life for me. My path to cartooning can be traced to an advertisement I read, "Draw your way to popularity, profit and girls! Be a cartoonist!" It's fair to say I was spectacularly misinformed.

SB: When did you first sell your art?
GS: As a kid, I sold my drawings and various creations door-to-door in my neighborhood. In junior high, I sold drawings of naked women in the libray during lunch. But, after getting busted several times I went legit and started selling pen and ink watercolor drawings of people's homes (to buy a bike). Then I struck a deal with a real estate agency to buy my illustrations as gifts for home owners. My parents would drive around town and find me sitting on curbs sketching houses until the sun went down. I was the kid who put on plays, magic shows and neighborhood carnivals. I also contributed editorial cartoons to the local newspaper. So, I've always seen my art as commerce. The trick today, is finding a paying audience, which is a challenge since the internet has dramatically altered the publishing industry.

Rapid Fire...

SB: Let's try something different now. Finish the following sentences: I draw in the style I do because...
GS: All the other styles were taken.

SB: The hardest part of cartooning is...
GS: Spending all the money.

SB: I admire...
GS: The inventors of the potato peeler and salad spinner.

SB: When I'm having a hard time coming up with ideas...
GS: I'm sorry, I'm not familiar with that sensation.

SB: I deal with rejection...
GS: Through righteous indignation, self-medication and phone calls to friends who support and enable my delusions of grandeur.

SB: Oh, I know it! Most cartoonists...
GS: Have IQs greater than their bank balance (also, they taste like chicken).

SB: When I'm not cartooning...
GS: I'm defending my choices and fighting with the person I could've been.

SB: My advice for aspiring cartoonists is.
GS: (1) Marry young while your youthful optimism is still sexy. (2) Learn to cook.

In Closing

SB: I like cartooning because...

GS: I can say what I feel and communicate it with others fairly quickly - even without words, which can't be said of many art forms. In a flash, you can make a person laugh, touch their heart, or present them an alternative side to an issue. Cartoons can be like poetry or haiku in the sense that so much is captured and conveyed in a few seconds. All you need is a pen and paper. Anyone who uses their creativity knows the rush of excitement when you successfully work out an idea - it's a celebration of lightning striking; a magical, self-satisfied feeling. There's nothing like it.

SB: What experiences have influenced you as a cartoonist?

GS: Selling seeds door-to-door, bartending for celebrities, being a life guard, swim instructor, dish washer, insurance salesman, moving man for dead peoples' stuff, singing telegrams (dressed as a penguin), actor, model, waiter, security guard, financial consultant, rubber band warehouse worker, Census taker, carpenter, party staffer, color copy engineer, an abundance of original sin, and living in New York City and Los Angeles have all served to twist my mind.

SB: Thank you for your insights into cartooning, Graham. Now, one last question...
If you weren't a cartoonist, what could you see yourself doing?

GS: Putting the red plastic strips on slices of baloney.

MAN VS MARGUERITA

Also by Graham:
www.GRAHAMALE.COM

GAG CARTOONS

DOG CARTOONS

POLICIAL CARTOONS

A NEW CHRISTMAS CLASSIC

BONELESS CHUCK®

Boneless Chuck is my proudest creation. He is loved around the world. His journey and the letters and photos he receives from fans will amaze you. 10% of his sales are donated to help those with cancer pay their daily bills.

POLICIAL CARTOONS

Greeting cards, mugs, t-shirts, and more!

Laughter.
The vaccination for any situation.

Stop the World
I Want to
Get Off

Laughter in the time of Covid

The Art of Survival
By GRAHAM SALE

Coming Soon!
Sign up to be notified when it is released.
www.GRAHAMSALE.COM

Made in the USA
Columbia, SC
22 October 2021